Under Your Nose
A Book About Nature's Gifts

Judith and **Shandley McMurray**
Foreword by **Robert Bateman**

Original art by Robert Bateman
with
The Tobin Island Artists
D. A. Dunford
Karen Genovese
Susan Gosevitz
Loretta Rogers
Darcey Sills

Simon Dunford, Junior Member
Megan Torisawa, Junior Member

Guest Artists
Dwight Aranha, Brad Bateman, Andy Donato

FIREFLY BOOKS

A FIREFLY BOOK

Published by Firefly Books Ltd. 2015
Copyright © 2015 Firefly Books Ltd.
Text copyright © 2015 Children's Books For Charity
Art copyright © 2015 Permission to use art in this book granted to Children's Books for Charity

Second printing

Publisher Cataloging-in-Publication Data (U.S.)
A CIP record for this title is available from Library of Congress

Library and Archives Canada Cataloguing in Publication
A CIP record for this title is available from Library and Archives Canada

Published in the United States by
Firefly Books (U.S.) Inc.
P.O. Box 1338, Ellicott Station
Buffalo, New York 14205

Published in Canada by
Firefly Books Ltd.
50 Staples Avenue, Unit 1
Richmond Hill, Ontario L4B 0A7

Cover and interior design by Hartley Millson
Front cover by Robert Bateman
Back cover by Susan Gosevitz
Artwork photographed by Martin Kaspers Photography,
Peter Gatt Photography, Scott Turnbull Photography

Printed in Canada

The publisher gratefully acknowledges the financial support for our publishing program by the Government of Canada through the Canada Book Fund as administered by the Department of Canadian Heritage.

For Michaelya and Cambria
Judith McMurray

For Marley and Pierce
Shandley McMurray

Proceeds from the sale of this book will be donated to The Bateman Foundation and the Canadian Wildlife Foundation

Robert Bateman ▶

Foreword

In the past, children spent most of their free time playing out in nature. Today, the average young person spends seven hours a day, seven days a week, staring at the screen of a television, computer or handheld device. Technology has provided great opportunities and conveniences, but in too many cases it has also become an addiction.

Studies of various cultures have shown that connecting with nature is not only educational for children but therapeutic as well. There is great joy in learning all that nature can teach us.

In *Under Your Nose*, two children panic when faced with a vacation without their electronic gadgets. Left to their own devices, they explore the wonders of the world around them and discover that the beauty of nature is something to cherish and protect.

—*Robert Bateman*

Under Your Nose

Today we're driving to Nana and Gramps' cottage for seven days. We'll be without my parents and, even worse, without television! Sitting in the back seat I turn on my tablet while my sister, Chloe, puts on her pink earphones and turns her music up so loud the cars next to us can probably hear.

After a long drive Gramps points to a sparkling waterfall and says, "Turn off those gadgets. We're close."

A few minutes later we pull into the cottage's long driveway. "Here we are," says Nana.

D. A. Dunford

"Zachary," Gramps says, "give me a hand with these bags."

Now that I'm seven, I'm strong enough to carry two bags. Chloe's nine, but for some reason she can only carry her pillow and a book.

I open the screen door to the cottage, walk through the living room and say hi to Monty, the moose painting that hangs over the fireplace. Then I climb the creaky wooden stairs to the room Chloe and I share.

Chloe takes her tablet into the hall and yells over the banister. "Nana, do we have Wi-Fi here?"

"Why what?" Nana asks from somewhere downstairs.

Karen Genovese

We clean all afternoon—dusting, scrubbing and sweeping until Nana calls us for dinner.

After we eat, Chloe and I play games on our tablets until a loud boom rocks the cottage. It's so powerful Chloe jumps in her seat.

A flash of lightning brightens the room. "What was that?" I ask, trying to sound calm.

"Thunder," Gramps says. "It just sounds louder on the lake because the noise bounces off the rocky cliffs and carries over the water."

Then the lights flicker and go out completely. It's so dark I can barely see my hands.

Nana hands us some flashlights. "Let's go to bed," she says. "I'm sure the lights will come on by morning."

D. A. Dunford ▶

D.A.Dunford

The next morning I sneak out of the bedroom, trying not to wake Chloe.

"Morning," Gramps says. "I'm going to the dock. Want to come?"

I follow him down the rocky path. From the dock I hear Chloe yell as she runs from the cottage to join us. "The power is still out. And our tablets aren't charged! What are we going to do now?"

"I've spent every summer of my life here without gadgets," says Gramps. "We have nature's playground at our doorstep and plenty to do. Just look over there."

I turn to see a family of mallard ducks paddling past the dock, the fluffy babies swimming in a line beside their mother.

Megan Torisawa

☐ Moss
☐ Caterpillar
☐ Pinecone
☐ Squirrel
☐ Stream
☐ Deer
☐ Rocks
☐ Frog
☐ Dragonfly
☐ 4 Types of Leaves

Megan Torisawa

After breakfast Gramps takes Chloe and me into the woods and gives us a piece of paper and pencil. "Time for a scavenger hunt," he says. "I want you to find moss, a caterpillar, a pinecone, a squirrel, a stream, a deer, rocks, a frog, a dragonfly and leaves. Draw pictures of the things you can't bring back."

Up ahead, a branch snaps. A family of deer! I'm about to sit down and draw them when Gramps says, "Don't sit on the deer berries!"

"What?" I ask.

"Poop," he laughs, pointing to a pile of small, brown berries on the ground. "Deer droppings look like berries. Trust me, you don't want to eat one!" He turns back towards the cottage and says, "Holler if you need anything. I won't be far."

Robert Bateman ▶

Robert Bateman

Just as Gramps disappears from sight a prickly pinecone hits me on the head. I look up and spot a red squirrel sitting on a tree branch. I put the pinecone in my pocket and check it off the list.

Chloe and I approach a stream with a pile of branches in the middle. Two beavers place the sticks on the pile and use mud to hold them in place.

"That looks like fun. Why don't we make our own dam?" I say to Chloe.

We spend the rest of the morning putting branches in the stream and squishing mud and moss between them. By the time we finish, we're covered in muck.

"Let's go back and show Gramps how many things we've found." Chloe says.

Loretta Rogers

◀ Loretta Rogers

*I*t seems like we've been walking forever but we still haven't found the cottage. The farther into the woods we go, the darker it gets, and all of the trees look the same.

Robert Bateman

Chloe slips her hand into mine. I remember a show on television that said moss grows thicker on the north side of a tree. The compass on Gramps' car had shown an N when we drove into the driveway. All we have to do is follow the moss and we won't go in circles. Hopefully we'll find our way back to the cottage.

I grab a clump of moss for a closer look. "What's that?" Chloe asks, picking some grey pellets from the fuzzy green pile in my hand.

"I don't know. Let's ask Gramps when we get back."

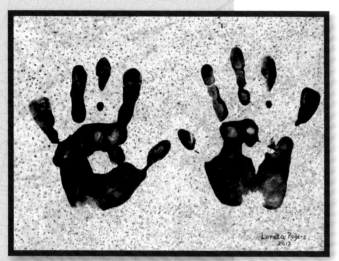
Loretta Rogers

"**Y**ou're certainly muddy!" Nana says when we arrive back at the cottage. "Where have you been?"

"We got a bit lost," Chloe says, smiling. "But look at what we have."

We've found everything on Gramps' list except for a caterpillar and a dragonfly. Gramps studies Chloe's pellets. "These are owl pellets," he says, pulling one apart. Inside are tiny pieces of fur. "Owls swallow their food whole and digest everything except bones and fur, which they cough up into a little pellet."

Chloe doesn't want them, but I think they're cool, so I put the pellets in a jar to bring home.

Susan Gosevitz ▶

Simon Dunford

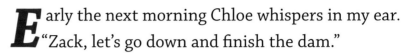arly the next morning Chloe whispers in my ear. "Zack, let's go down and finish the dam."

Our tablets are on the counter as we tiptoe downstairs but we don't stop to check if they're charged. We quietly shut the door behind us and a bird greets us with a sweet song. It sounds as if the bird is saying, "Where are you?" and answering, "Here I am."

"That's a red-eyed vireo," comes Gramps' voice from behind us. I jump with surprise. "You can tell by his unique song and red eyes. Want to feed him?"

"Sure," I say, taking a colourful caterpillar from Gramps' hand but the bird flies away.

"Maybe next time." Gramps chuckles as he walks away. "Try not to get lost today."

Susan Gosevitz ▶

Loretta Rogers

Back at the dam, Chloe and I get to work adding more branches, mud and moss, making it bigger and stronger.

Our little dam is full of life. A bullfrog lets out a deep croak before jumping off one of the branches. A dragonfly swoops down to the water. His body looks like an airplane but his feet hang below like a basket, ready to catch mosquitoes. We take a break to draw it—the last item on our list.

As we sit by the side of the stream, a damselfly rests on my knee, folding his sparkling wings over a shiny black body. He stays only a few seconds before darting off to join his friend for a dance over the water.

Darcey Sills ▶

Darcey Sills

Gramps is outside when we arrive back at the cottage. "Good news. The power's back and I plugged in your gadgets. Want them?" he asks.

"No thanks," we say together. "We've got something to show you," I add.

We lead Nana and Gramps into the woods. When our dam comes into view, Nana gasps. "This looks just like it was made by beavers!"

"I'm impressed," Gramps says as he takes our picture. "You two made an excellent home for the forest creatures. I told you that nature provides the best playground. Was I right or what?"

"You were right," Chloe admits, giving him a hug.

◀ Darcey Sills

25

W̲e spend the rest of the afternoon at the cottage playing cards and eating popcorn. After dinner Gramps hands me a flashlight. "It's time for a nighttime adventure," he announces.

As we step outside I hear a bird sing and I stop to listen. The bird sounds like it's saying, "Who cooks for you?"

"That's a barred owl," Gramps says. "The most handsome bird around, and the one with the most interesting call."

As we turn back towards the cottage a loud slap rings through the trees.

"What was that?" Chloe stammers.

"Just a beaver slapping his tail," Gramps says. "They do that to warn other beavers that something's approaching. You'll know the beaver has seen you if you hear that sound!"

Robert Bateman

*B*ack at the cottage, Gramps leads us to the fire pit near the dock. It's filled with little sticks, woodchips and a bit of newspaper. He lights a match and holds it to the paper. Within a minute the wood's crackling.

"I know how to make this fire even better," Chloe says, running up to the house.

She returns with Nana, arms filled with marshmallows, graham crackers and chocolate. I tear open the marshmallow bag, popping one in my mouth before loading another onto a stick.

Once it's perfectly golden, I sandwich my gooey masterpiece between two crackers and a square of chocolate. As I take a bite, the marshmallow sticks to my lips and chocolate dribbles down my chin.

"This is s'morelicious," I say and everyone laughs.

Andy Donato

◀ D. A. Dunford

After we wash up Nana tucks us into bed. My arms and legs feel so heavy that they sink into the mattress.

"Thanks for bringing us here," Chloe says between yawns. "I loved building our dam."

"Gramps really knows a lot about nature. Maybe tomorrow he can take us out in the canoe so we can get a closer look at the ducks." I add.

"What a wonderful day you two have had exploring the world of nature that's been right under your nose all along." Nana says. "Who would have guessed you wouldn't miss your tablets!"

Andy Donato ▶

Did You Know?

1. **Bald Eagles** aren't actually bald. They are called that because "bald" meant white many, many years ago. They don't grow their fancy white head and tail feathers until they turn five.

2. **Mallard ducks** shed their feathers twice a year. They can't fly until all of their new feathers grow in, which takes weeks.

3. Male **white-tailed deer** are called bucks. They grow beautiful antlers once a year but they fall off in the winter.

4. Female **pinecones** are big and spiky while male pinecones tend to be smaller and closed in.

5. The **beaver** is the national symbol of Canada. Its teeth never stop growing, so it needs to chew on branches and cut down trees to keep them from getting too long.

6. **Red-eyed vireos** spend most of their time flitting between the tops of trees, making them difficult to spot.

7. Made of sticks and mud, **beaver dams** block the flow of water on one side and create a deep wetland on the other. The new section helps protect them from water-wary predators while allowing them a deep enough entry to their underwater lodges.

8. **Barred owls** often make their homes in large cavities in trees. When this isn't possible, however, they will sometimes claim empty hawk or even squirrel nests.

9. There are over 200 different species of **squirrels** in the world. None of them live in Australia. The African pygmy squirrel is the world's smallest, measuring only five inches long. The largest, known as the Indian giant squirrel, can grow up to three feet long.

10. A **dragonfly**'s wing measures between two to five inches today. Fossils of dragonfly ancestors from 300 million years ago, however, prove that the once-monstrous creatures boasted wings up to two and a half feet long.

11. While more vividly coloured than a dragonfly, **damselflies** are often smaller, more delicate and weaker fliers. Some species lay their eggs underwater, with the female staying submerged for up to an hour.

12. The most common place to find a **caterpillar** is on the underside of a leaf attached to a vein. They prefer to feed at night, so bring a flashlight.

13. **Thunder** is the sound caused by **lightning**. Lightning is so hot (about 20,000 degrees Celsius) that it heats the air, causing a sonic shock wave. Because light is faster than sound (about a million times in fact) we see lightning before we hear thunder. After you see lightning, count the number of seconds until the thunder arrives — for every four seconds you count between the light and the boom, the storm is one mile away.

14. It takes between two and four years for a tadpole to grow into a fully formed **bullfrog**.